ACKNOWLEDGEMENT OF COUNTRY

Budyari naady'unya dhiyi Dharug ngurawa.
Good to see you here on Dharug Country.
Ngaradyingun dali Darug yiyura,
We acknowledge and pay respect to the Darug people,
ngaan yiyura dali diyi ngurang birang.
the traditional Aboriginal custodians of this land.
Yanma muday Ngurrawa diyi nangamayi marri.
Please tread softly on our ancient lands because our dreaming is forever.

MAP OF DHARUG COUNTRY

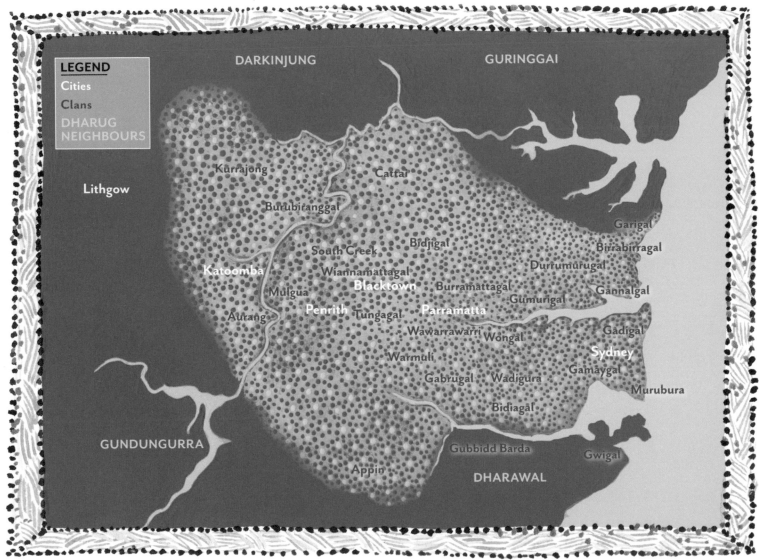

LEGEND
Cities
Clans
DHARUG NEIGHBOURS

DARKINJUNG

GURINGGAI

Lithgow

Kurrajong

Cattai

Burubiranggal

Garigal

Bidjigal

Birrabirragal

South Creek

Durrumurugal

Katoomba

Wiannamattagal

Blacktown

Burramattagal

Gannalgal

Mulgua

Gumurigal

Penrith

Tungagal

Parramatta

Aurang

Wawarrawarri

Wongal

Gadigal

Warmuli

Sydney

Gabrugal

Wadigura

Gamaygal

Bidiagal

Murubura

GUNDUNGURRA

Gubbidd Barda

Gwigal

Appin

DHARAWAL

This map shows some of the clans of the Darug people.
This map is a guide only. Boundaries are not set lines, but shared areas.

Acknowledgement of Country text (Dharug and English) and Dharug map
© Jasmine Seymour and Leanne Mulgo Watson

Found in Sydney

A Counting Adventure

Joanne O'Callaghan

illustrated by Kori Song

ALLEN&UNWIN
SYDNEY·MELBOURNE·AUCKLAND·LONDON

1

One giant aeroplane comes in to land

A boy looking lost and a helping hand

Welcome to TARONGA ZOO

2

Two baby koalas sleep in a tree

Kangaroos, emus and giraffes to see

3

Three cheeky seagulls are flying around

Careful your hot chips don't fall on the ground!

4

Four yellow rubber ducks sit down below

And a toy you can shake then watch it snow

5

Five boats are sailing at sunset tonight

See the movie screen, so big and so bright

6

Six dogs of all sizes walking the track

Bronte to Bondi and all the way back

7

Seven tall surfboards stand straight in a row

Time for our lesson now? Come on, let's go!

8

Eight glowing lanterns; a hole in the wall

A friendship garden with a waterfall

9

Nine people wave from a bridge you can climb

A view to remember for all of time
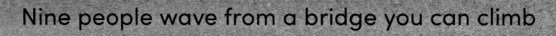

10

Ten children playing; they jump, slide and run
Centennial Park is a lot of fun!

11

Eleven sea creatures behind the glass

A manta ray, turtle and shark swim past

12

Twelve painted faces look down from the walls

What else is hiding in these rooms and halls?

100

One hundred buildings spread under our feet

And a rooftop pool to escape the heat

1000

One thousand gum trees grow up to the sky

Where mountains are blue and extremely high

1,000,000

One million tiles gleaming bright in the sun

Sydney Opera House is for everyone

This is a city loved by all who come

Magnificent fireworks, so much fun

Friends to meet, incredible sights to see

Spectacular Sydney, the place to be!

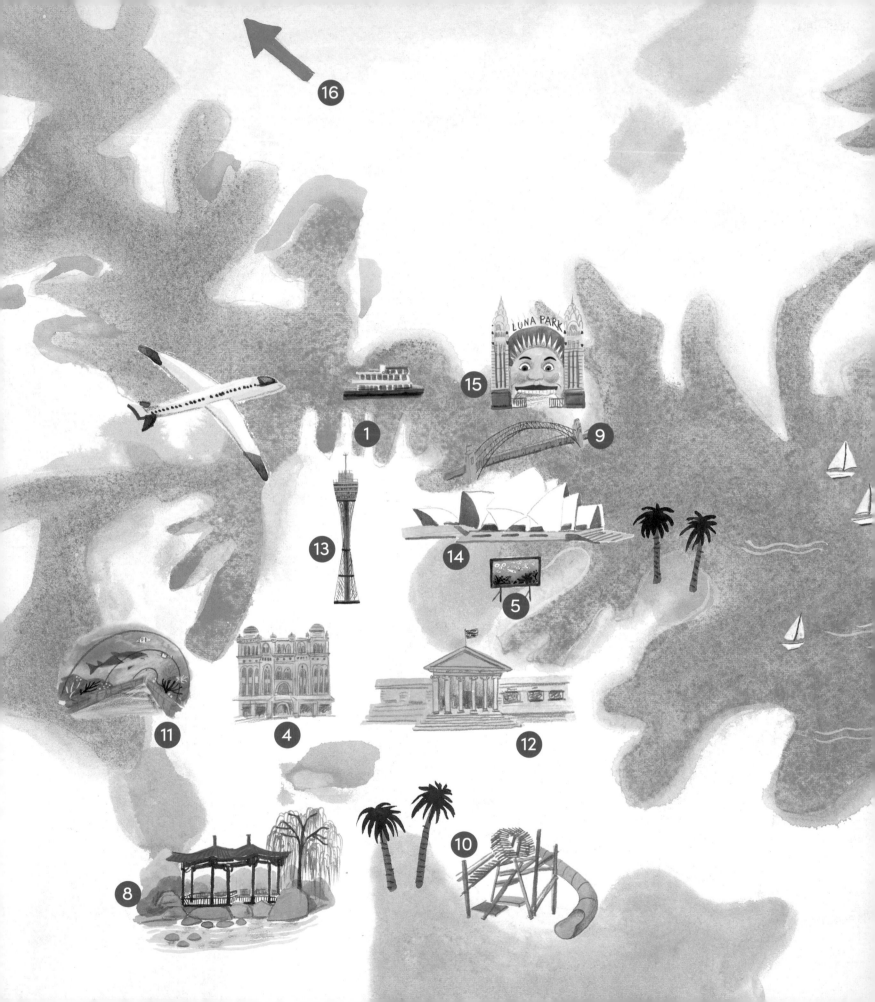

EXPLORE SYDNEY

DID YOU KNOW?

There are actually more kangaroos in Australia than there are humans. Wow!

People from all around the world call Sydney home. Languages spoken by Sydneysiders include English, Mandarin, Arabic, Cantonese, Vietnamese and Greek. There are also many Indigenous languages spoken by First Australians.

Sydney Harbour is the world's largest natural harbour and home to dolphins, turtles and sea dragons.

Sydney has over 100 beaches. 'Nippers' are kids who learn about the beach and lifesaving.

The Chinese Garden of Friendship was a gift to Sydney from its Chinese sister city of Guangzhou.

The curved roof of the Sydney Opera House is covered in 1,056,006 tiles. These were made in Sweden and shipped to Sydney.

In 1932, nine-year-old Lennie Gwyther rode his chestnut pony, Ginger Mick, from Victoria to Sydney to see the opening of the Sydney Harbour Bridge. He travelled 1000 kilometres alone, over 33 days.

Budding artists between the ages of 5 and 18 can submit a portrait to the Art Gallery of NSW as part of the Young Archie Competition.

To listen to Joanne O'Callaghan and Kevin Yang read this book in English and Mandarin, please scan the QR code or go to www.allenandunwin.com/found-in-sydney

Explore Melbourne next!

简体中文版同步出售
Also available in Simplified Chinese

For Bong, forever in friendship. JO

To Bong, who always saw the darkness but led me to
explore the brightness of the world. KS

First published by Allen & Unwin in 2023

Allen & Unwin
Cammeraygal Country
83 Alexander Street, Crows Nest NSW 2065 Australia
Phone: (61 2) 8425 0100
Email: info@allenandunwin.com
Web: www.allenandunwin.com

Allen & Unwin acknowledges the Traditional Owners of the Country on which we live and work.
We pay our respects to all Aboriginal and Torres Strait Islander Elders, past and present.

 A catalogue record for this
book is available from the
National Library of Australia

ISBN (English) 978 1 76052 624 5
ISBN (Simplified Chinese) 978 1 76052 626 9

For teaching resources, explore www.allenandunwin.com/resources/for-teachers

Illustration technique: opaque watercolour, collage, coloured pencils, crayons, pastels
Cover and text design by Sandra Nobes
Set in 18 pt Sofia Pro Regular
Colour reproduction by Splitting Image, Wantirna, Victoria
This book was printed in August 2022 by C&C Offset Printing Co. Ltd, China

1 3 5 7 9 10 8 6 4 2

 MIX
Paper | Supporting
responsible forestry
FSC® C008047

www.joanneocallaghan.com
www.korisong.com